The Super Fuel Secret

Written by Frank Pedersen
Illustrated by Paul Könye

Contents

Meet the Characters

Dr Dee Hashida

An energy research scientist.

Shozuri Akara

Dee's boss, in charge of the Hatsumira Corporation.

Ramirez

A shady secret agent.

The Silent Man

Another secret agent who never speaks.

Dear Reader

If you had the choice between making huge amounts of money, or making a new fuel that could help save our environment, which would you choose? Here's a mystery story about a scientist who discovers something amazing ... and then gets the surprise of her life!

Frank Pedersen
Author

Global Locator

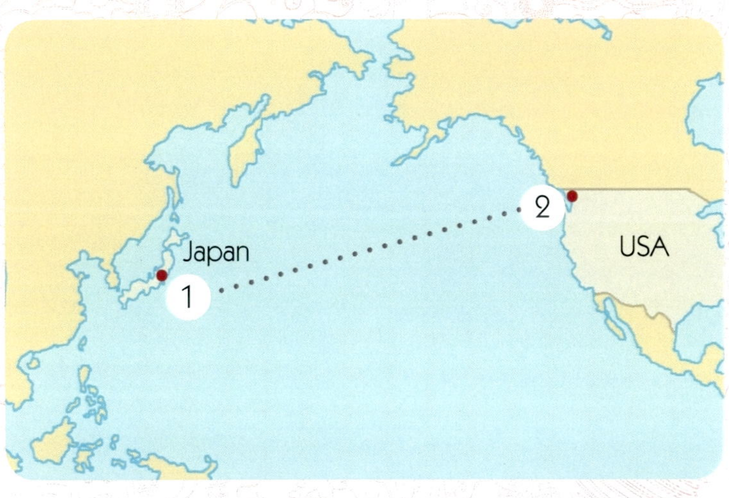

1. Akara's office in Tokyo
2. Dee's lab in Seattle

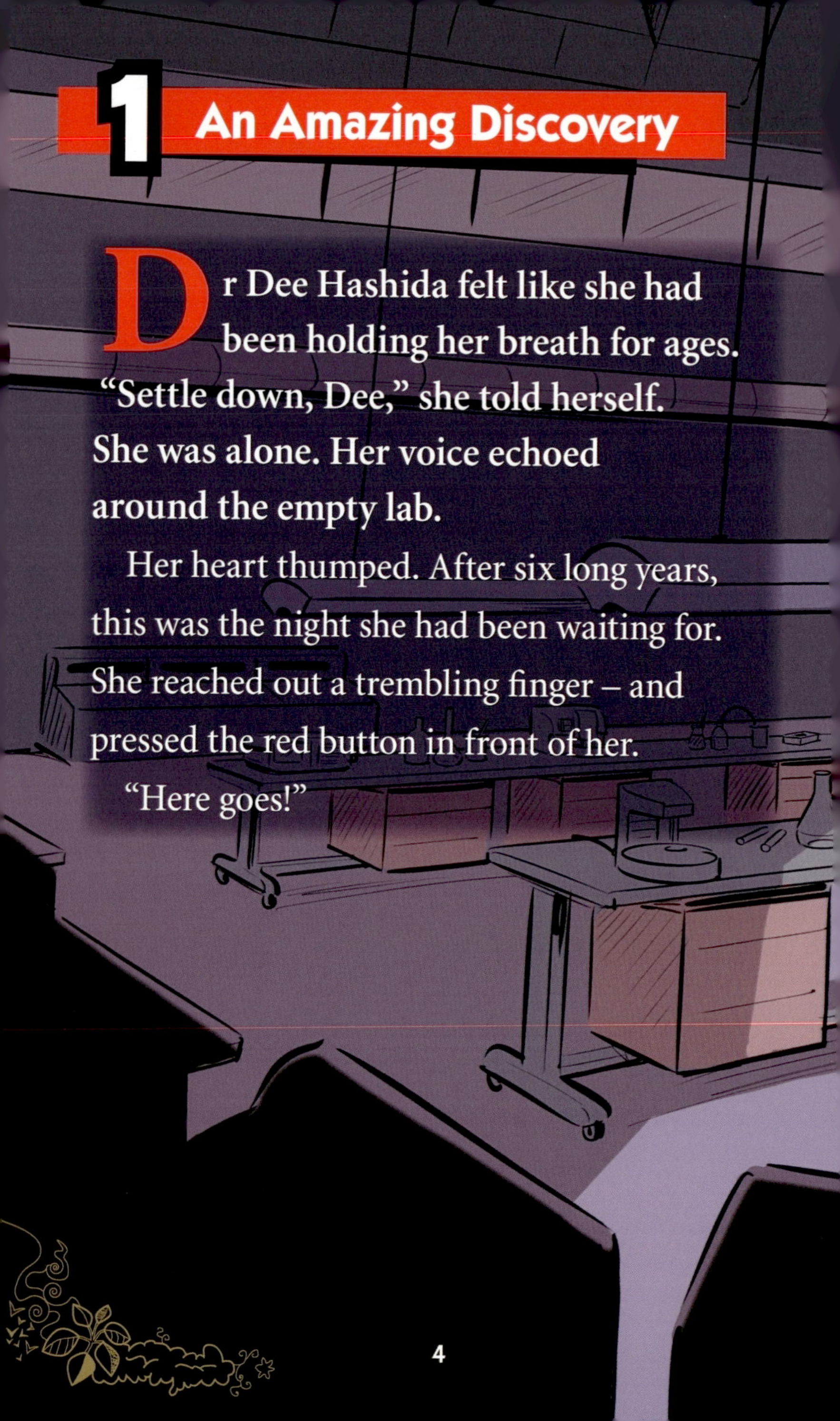

1 An Amazing Discovery

Dr Dee Hashida felt like she had been holding her breath for ages. "Settle down, Dee," she told herself. She was alone. Her voice echoed around the empty lab.

Her heart thumped. After six long years, this was the night she had been waiting for. She reached out a trembling finger – and pressed the red button in front of her.

"Here goes!"

For one crazy moment, she felt like there should have been a burst of music. Instead there was nothing – just a low hum and an eerie blue glow from the computer in front of her.

It was just what Dee had been hoping for. An icy chill crept down her spine. In a few seconds, she would know if her work had been successful.

Far away, the Hatsumira Corporation Skytower rose into the Tokyo sky.

On the 47th floor of the Skytower, a grey-faced man shut the book he had been reading. He looked at the neon lights of the city. It was late, and he wished he was in bed, asleep. But he wasn't – and he knew what he had to do next.

He took a deep breath and punched a number into his phone.

"Ramirez," he said softly. "We have a problem."

Back in Dee's lab, a minute seemed to stretch into an hour. The data from her experiment slowly printed out.

She closed her eyes and picked up the results. She had done this experiment before. Every time it had failed.

But this time …

There could well have been a burst of music. Dee wouldn't have noticed. Her eyes were glued to the number at the bottom of the sheet.

"I don't believe it," she said. "It can't be true."

Suddenly, everything had changed.

2 Everything Changes

Everything had changed.
The man inside the car folded his phone shut. Another man sat beside him. The car drove silently around the corner and stopped.

The two men looked up at the building in front of them. A lone light burned in a window, nine floors up.

The men exchanged a glance. One nodded, and they both opened their doors.

Dee could barely think. She rechecked the results. She shook her head. There could be no doubt.

She touched the trackpad on her laptop. The screen lit up. She clicked on her email program and sat staring at it.

She smiled. She had dreamt of sending this email for years – and now she couldn't think of what to say!

"You're a scientist, Dee," she said. "Just tell it like it is."

She began to type.

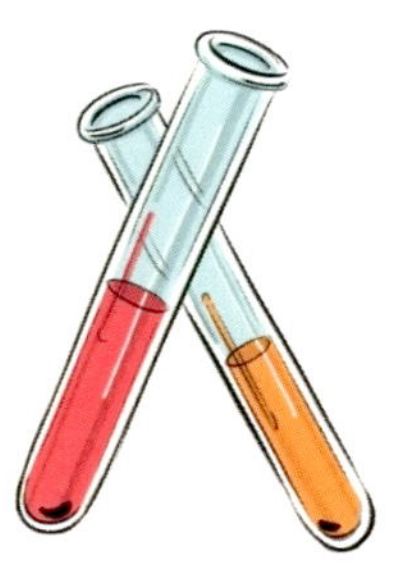

On the 47th floor of the Skytower, the low sound of a Japanese flute filled the office.

Dr Akara, the grey man in the chair, opened his eyes. It meant he had an email.

He clicked his computer.

"To Dr Akara," said the email. **"Tonight, at 9.35 pm, a new experiment was done, with lower energy inputs. This time, we got a POSITIVE result."**

Akara's face was still, but his heart fell. This was not good.

"If these results are right, this will be big news. It will mean an endless source of energy – a super fuel made from water. A super fuel that will not make greenhouse gases, but steam instead.

With kind regards, Dee Hashida."

Akara opened his phone. "I need an email block," he said. "Nothing is to go in or out."

He gave Dee's email address to the person he had called. She was now cut off from the virtual world.

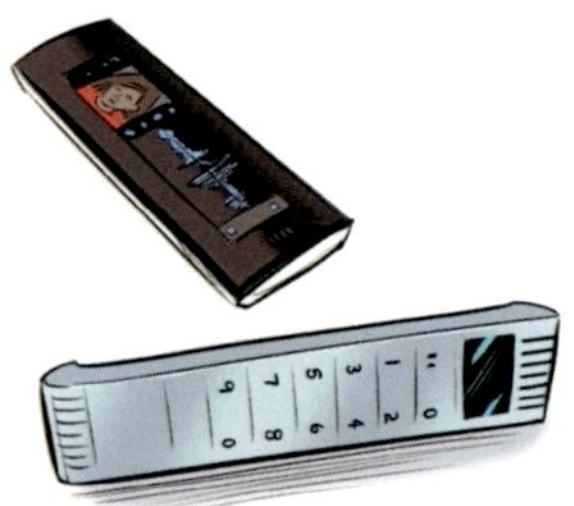

The two men started up the stairs.
Stairs were safer than lifts. Lifts had security cameras, and there was to be no record, anywhere, of their visit.

“At least it’s only nine floors up,” said the first man.

“I don’t mind walking up,” replied the other. “Carrying someone nine floors down is the hard part.”

3 A New Super Fuel

Dee thought about her work. If people could just split water into hydrogen and oxygen, they would have an endless supply of energy.

For years, scientists had been trying to find a way to achieve this – and now she, Dee Hashida, had done it.

Global warming, climate change, fossil fuels, high petrol prices – now, all these problems could be fixed.

Everyone could have a free super fuel to help them power their homes, farms and work.

And the only waste would be more water!

Akara was busy. Even for the boss of the Hatsumira Corporation, making a bank transfer of 25 million dollars was not easy.

"You should be used to it by now," he sighed. He found the online form on his computer. He keyed in a password and held his thumb on the fingerprint reader.

"Transaction OK," said the text on the screen.

"Third floor," grunted the first man. "Only another four to go."

His companion nodded grimly, and cracked his knuckles.

Their footsteps on the stairs were like the ticking of an alarm clock, counting down.

Dee knew that she should go home and try to get some rest. But she also knew that she would not fall asleep.

Instead, she set about telling the world about her discovery.

She emailed her lab staff. She emailed other researchers. She emailed her friends. She sent copies of the results. By the time dawn had broken, the news of her breakthrough would be across the globe.

There would be discussions and disagreements, of course. Scientists around the

world would rush to try and copy her results for themselves, just to see if this simple super fuel worked. But, after years of trying and testing, Dee was sure.

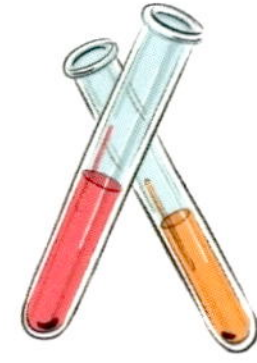

"Are you sure?" asked Akara.

"Yes," came the voice on the other end of the phone. "Increased email traffic from the blocked address. All deleted."

Akara hung up, and dialled another number.

The phone buzzed. The man felt in his pocket and checked the caller ID.

He opened the phone and listened.

"Yes," he said. He looked at the nearby sign. "We're on the sixth floor."

Thirty seconds later, a knock on the lab door almost made Dee jump out of her skin. She was used to late nights alone in her lab, and no one had ever come up before.

"Calm down, Dee," she said aloud. "These late nights are making you jumpy. It's probably just the security guys checking that I'm OK."

She checked the "sending" bar for her latest emails, and went to the lab door.

A Difficult Choice

That night, Tokyo was the last place that Dee had expected to end up.

After her surprise at seeing her lab assistant, Ramirez, at the door so late, she relaxed. It did seem a little strange that she and Ramirez, and this other man who she didn't know, had been called to head office. Perhaps her very first email of the night had been read by her boss, Chief Research Officer Akara.

On the tiny jet, Ramirez was quiet. Dee guessed it was just because it was late. During the two-hour flight, the other man sat behind her, saying nothing.

A black car waited for them at the airport. In the early hours of the morning, Tokyo's traffic was light. Within an hour, Dee could see the Hatsumira Skytower, above the rest of the city's buildings. And in ten minutes, she was riding the glass lift towards the 47th floor.

Ramirez and the other man stared straight ahead. Dee dared not look down. Lifts with glass floors made her feel nervous.

And she was getting a bad feeling from her surroundings.

"Dee, what a pleasure," said the grey-faced man. "Welcome to the Hatsumira Corporation."

Dee went into Akara's office, and the door closed behind her. Ramirez and the silent man had stayed outside.

"Mr Akara," she nodded politely. "It's nice to see you again. I …"

Akara raised his hand, and smiled.

"Dr Hashida," he said. "I'm sure you have many questions. But first, let me congratulate you on your discovery."

Dee felt relieved. Akara had got her email, after all. That's what all this was about, of course.

"I'm thrilled," said Dee, with a smile. "This has huge potential for our planet."

Akara smiled his grey smile.

"Yes," he said. "But before we go any further, please let me show you something."

Akara led Dee to a room near his office, and opened a curtain. Behind it was a steel security door. Akara keyed in a number on the security pad and the door clicked open.

"This looks like a prison cell," joked Dee.

"Please," said Akara with another smile, indicating that Dee should enter.

After a few seconds, Dee's eyes could see in the dim light. She looked around, and saw that this was a storage room, with shelves and shelves of dusty boxes, folders and files. In the middle of the room was a single table, with a laptop.

"What is this room?" said Dee, feeling very uneasy.

"Why, this is where we store humanity's wildest dreams and most heartfelt wishes," said Akara in a voice that made Dee shudder. He pointed to a file. "In that file is the cure for the common cold. This box," he continued, moving down the shelf, "contains everything needed to rid the world of malaria mosquitoes."

Dee stared at Akara. Was he mad?

"Here, we have an endless source of electricity, based on using Earth's magnetic field," he said, blowing dust off a folder. "This is one of my favourites – a genetically modified rice plant that can spread like a weed, and grow anywhere, any time." He shook his head. "We could fix hunger with a single batch of seeds."

"But …" said Dee, stunned. Akara held up his hand again and smiled.

"And here we have a whole shelf, just for cheap fuels. We have lots of them – but we've left a space for you."

Dee felt like she had fallen all 47 floors to the ground. She could only utter one word.

"Why?"

Akara shrugged his shoulders. "We are the biggest corporation in the world. We make billions out of pills and potions that people buy when they catch a cold. We sell billions of dollars of malaria drugs. We own most of the electricity plants, and sell the power for billions. We produce billions of dollars worth of fertilisers and pesticides for farmers to spread on their crops. We own most of the

world's oil and petrol refineries. Why would we want to have these problems solved?

"What would happen if everyone around the world had their own super fuel, made from water? Do you know what that would do to our sales of oil and gas?"

Suddenly Dee felt angry.

"But you can't do that," she said. "That's inhumane! You're letting people – and our planet – suffer just because you want to make money? I won't let you do that."

Akara smiled again. "It is always a hard choice," he said. "But you also have a hard choice to make." He pointed towards the table and the laptop.

Dee stared at the screen.

"Please check your bank account number," said Akara.

But Dee was looking at the other number on the screen. It was almost as long.

"Twenty-five million," she gasped.

"I will leave you to decide," said Akara softly. "All you need to do is press 'enter' and the transfer will be complete."

He went out of the room.

On the 47th floor, the grey-faced man sat in his chair, watching the city outside. Dawn was breaking, and a red sky was spreading in the east.

The roads and plazas below filled with cars, and their red lights made them seem like tiny veins, bringing the city to life.

He heard footsteps behind him, and turned in his chair.

"Dr Hashida," he smiled. "The world awakes to a beautiful morning. Have you made your choice?"

Dee looked out at the cityscape, stretching as far as the eye could see. She took a deep breath. "It is a beautiful morning," she replied. "And I have."

"And?" asked Akara.

And just as Dee had known it would, at the start of the longest night of her life, everything had changed. Hugely.

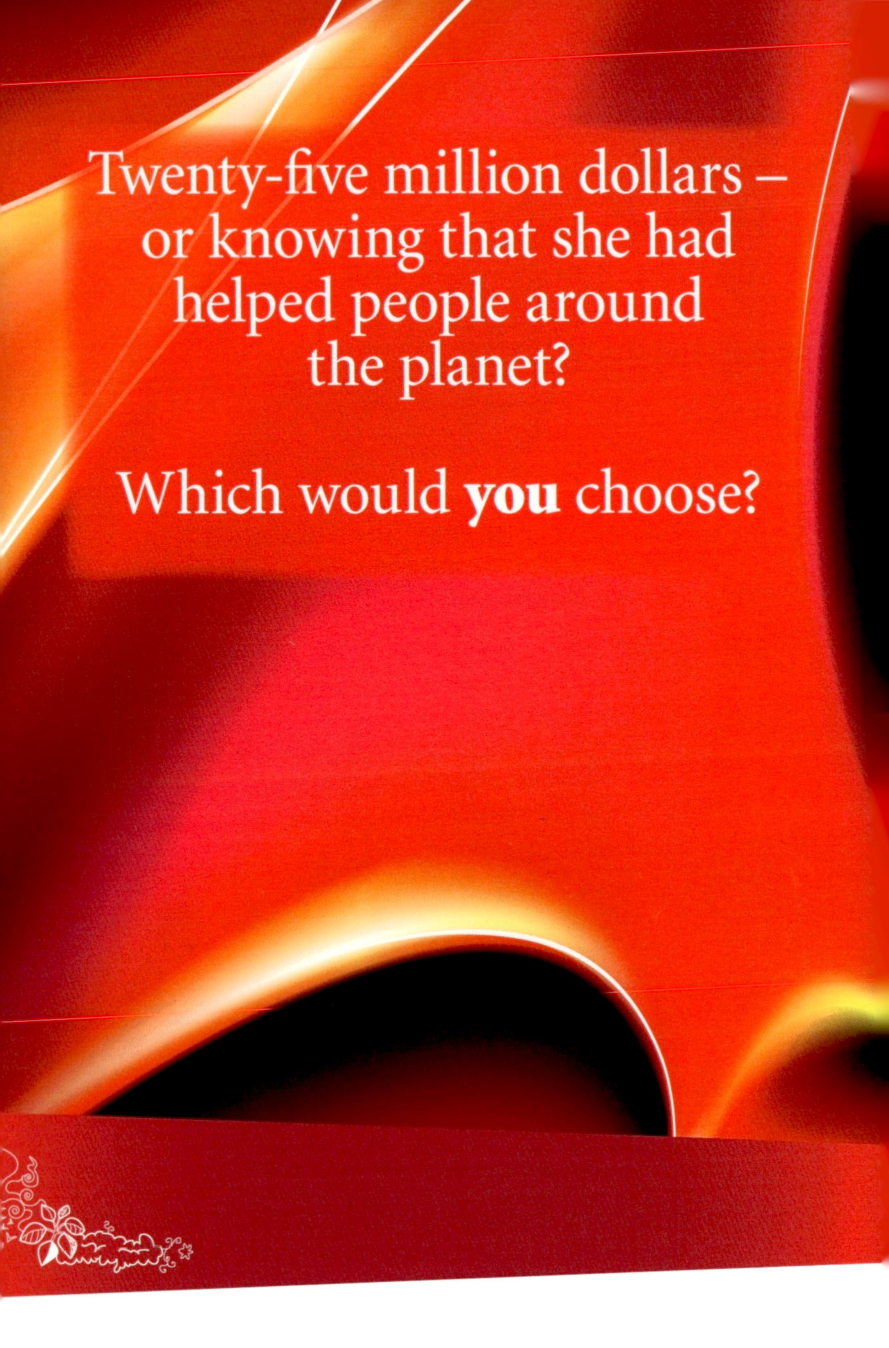
Twenty-five million dollars – or knowing that she had helped people around the planet?
Which would **you** choose?